# Calico Cat at School

written and illustrated by Donald Charles

**CP** CHILDRENS PRESS ™

CHICAGO

for Robin and Holly

Library of Congress Cataloging in Publication Data

Charles, Donald.
  Calico Cat at school.

  Summary: Calico Cat spends a day at school.
  [1.  School stories]   I.  Title.
PZ7.C374Cak     [E]      81-6096
ISBN 0-516-03445-6     AACR2

11 12 13 14 15 16 17 18 19 R 93 92 91

# Calico Cat
# at School

RING!

# Time to get up.

# Don't be late for school.

"Here I am on time,"
says Calico Cat.

# Start the day.

# Learn to read.

# Learn to write.

"It's fun to learn," says Calico Cat.

# "It's fun to run and play," says Calico Cat.

# Sing a song.

# Lunchtime:
## "It's fun to eat,"
## says Calico Cat.

# Storytime:
Calico Cat listens quietly.

# Calico Cat draws
a picture of himself.

School's out for today.
Hurry home.

# "See you tomorrow,"
says Calico Cat.

# Calico Cat can tell time.
# Can you?

7:30 a.m.
wake-up time

9:00 a.m.
school time

10:15 a.m.
recess time

12:00 noon
lunch time

2:30 p.m.
time to go home

8:30 p.m.
bed time

ABOUT THE AUTHOR/ARTIST

Donald Charles started his long career as an artist and author more than twenty-five years ago after attending the University of California and the Art League School of California. He began by writing and illustrating feature articles for the *San Francisco Chronicle,* and also sold cartoons and ideas to *The New Yorker* and *Cosmopolitan* magazines. Since then he has been, at various times. a longshoreman, ranch hand, truck driver, and editor of a weekly newspaper, all enriching experiences for a writer and artist. Ultimately he became creative director for an advertising agency, a post which he resigned several years ago to devote himself full-time to book illustration and writing. Mr. Charles has received frequent awards from graphic societies, and his work has appeared in numerous textbooks and periodicals.